WAKE UP, BABY BEAR!

Lynn Plourde

ILLUSTRATED BY

Teri Weidner

Down East Books

Camden, Maine

Down East Books

An imprint of The Rowman & Littlefield Publishing Group, Inc.
4501 Forbes Blvd., Ste. 200
Lanham, MD 20706
www.rowman.com

Distributed by NATIONAL BOOK NETWORK

Story copyright © 2018 Lynn Plourde
Illustrations copyright © 2018 Teri Weidner

Design by Piper Wallis

British Library Cataloguing-in-Publication Information available

Library of Congress Cataloging-in-Publication Data available

ISBN 978-1-60893-971-8 (hardcover)
ISBN 978-1-60893-972-5 (e-book)

♾™ The paper used in this publication meets the minimum requirements of American National Standard for Information Sciences—Permanence of Paper for Printed Library Materials, ANSI/NISO Z39.48-1992.

Printed in the United States of America

To Harrison,
such a sweet, caring cub.
—L.P.

For my talented friends in the
Portsmouth Illustrator's
Secret Society.
—T.W.

"Wake up, Baby Bear! It's spring!"
Mama Bear whispered in Baby Bear's ear.

But all she heard back from her baby black bear was **Zzzzzzzzzzz**!

"Wake up, Baby Bear!
No more hibernating
until next winter."
Papa Bear shook Baby Bear.

A louder **Zzzzzzzzzzzz**!

"He did stay up past his hibernating time last winter," said Papa Bear.
"Yes," agreed Mama Bear. "Let him sleep a **little** later.
His hungry belly will wake him up soon enough."

GRUMBLE!
Papa Bear laughed and patted his own belly.
"My hungry belly is loud enough
to wake up the whole forest.
I'm starved! Let's go find some food.
We can check on Baby Bear in a little while."

Baby Bear didn't answer
so Owl tickled Baby Bear's nose
with his feathers.

Soon after Mama and Papa
Bear left their den, there
was a **flap-flap** in the
doorway.

"Whoo-whoo! Whoo
is being a sleepy head?"
asked Owl.

AH—AH—AH—CHOOOOOOOO!
sneezed Baby Bear.

Then . . .
Zzzzzzzzzzzz!

Next there was a scrape-scrape as Moose tried to fit his antlers into the den.

"Wake. Up. Now."

Baby Bear didn't stir, so Moose nudged him with his antlers.

WHOP-WHOP-WHOP!
Baby Bear rolled out
of the den and
down the hill.

But still . . .
Zzzzzzzzzzzz!

Baby Bear didn't budge so Hare gave him a couple of little **jab-jabs** with his feet.

Then boing-boing—Hare hopped on over. "Rise and shine. It's spring! We've missed you, friend."

Baby Bear laughed—
HA! HEE! HO!

Those jabs must have tickled, but still . . .

Zzzzzzzzzzzz!

Owl, Moose, and Hare sighed.
"He's no fun," said Owl.
"Party pooper," said Moose.

"We'll have to celebrate spring
without him," said Hare,
as they headed off to frolic
in the fresh green world.

Still . . .

Zzzzzzzzzzzz!

Zzzzzzzzzzzz!

Zzzzzzzzzzzz!

Yeep! Yeep! **"Don't move!"**
Robin ordered Baby Bear.

But Baby Bear's belly moved up and down,
up and down, as he snored in and out, in and out.
Zzzzzzzzzzz! Zzzzzzzzzzz!

"Stop it! You'll spill my eggs!" screeched Robin.
Still . . . Zzzzzzzzzzz! **Zzzzzzzzzzz!**

So Robin did what any mother would do. She protected her little ones. Peck! Peck! She pecked Baby Bear right on the tip of his nose.

Zzzzz . . . **"OW!"** cried Baby Bear,
who finally woke up.

But as Baby Bear started
to get up, Robin pecked
him on the nose again
and said, "Don't move!
My eggs!"

Baby Bear looked in the direction Robin's wing was pointing and said, "Wow! Breakfast in bed—eggs! Thank you!"

Baby Bear licked his lips. Robin pecked his nose.

"Those are my babies, **not** your breakfast."

Just then Robin's nest started to slip. **Wibble-wobble-bobble!**

"Good catch. Thank you!" said Robin, warming up to this big furry creature who had saved her babies.

"Whoa!" cried Baby Bear as he caught the eggs in his paws.

"Now what?" asked Baby Bear, holding the eggs gently in his cupped paws.

But before Robin could answer . . .
crimple, crinkle, crackle!
Yeep, yeep, yeep!
Robin's eggs had cracked open.

"Awwww!" said Baby Bear.
"Your babies are soooo cute."

"Thank you," said Robin.
"But there's no time for admiring.
My babies need to eat."
Yeep, yeep, yeep!
The babies agreed.

"Will you babysit while I fetch them some food?"
GRUMBLE!
Just the mention of food made Baby Bear's belly growl
after going all winter without a meal. But still,
those babies needed watching so Baby Bear said,
"Don't worry, they're safe with me."

And they were safe.

And busy, busy, busy. **Yeep! Yeep! Yeep! Flit! Flitter! Flutter!**

Mama Robin came back

over

and over

and over again with food . . .

For **all** the babies.

Finally, after eating, it was time for a nap.

After all, they were only babies.

Just then, Mama Bear and Papa Bear returned.

Owl, Moose, and Hare returned.

They all shouted . . .

"WAKE UP, BABY BEAR!"

Yeep!

Yeep!

Yeep!

Zzzzzzzzzzz!

QUESTIONS ABOUT BLACK BEARS

(Check for the answers on the next page—**NO peeking!**)

1. There are eight kinds (species) of bears in the world. The American black bear is one kind. How many of the other seven species of bears can you name?

2. In which continent do American black bears live?

    A. South America
    B. North America
    C. Asia

3. Are black bears herbivores (plant eaters), carnivores (meat eaters), or omnivores (both plant and meat eaters)?

4. What's the name for a group of bears?

    A. a cuddle of bears
    B. a flock of bears
    C. a sloth of bears

5. How much weight do black bears lose over the winter when they are hibernating?

    A. 5-10% of their weight
    B. 25-40% of their weight
    C. They don't lose any weight

6. Do black bears drink when they are hibernating? Yes or no.

7. How old are black bear cubs when the mother bear shoos them away and won't protect them any more?

    A. 7 months old
    B. 17 months old
    C. 70 months old (or almost 6 years old)

8. When bears are awake and active, their hearts beat 80 to 100 times per minute, similar to a human heart. But when bears hibernate, their hearts slow down. How slow?

    A. 8-22 beats per minute
    B. 30-45 beats per minute
    C. 50-65 beats per minute

9. Do black bears like to hibernate in small or roomy dens (spaces)?

10. The average human lives to be 79 years old. What age does the average black bear live to?

    A. 25 years
    B. 50 years
    C. 75 years

ANSWERS

1. Brown bear, polar bear, giant panda, spectacled (also called Andean) bear, sloth bear, sun bear, Asiatic black bear

2. American black bears live in North America **(B)**— as far south as Mexico and Florida and as far north as Canada and Alaska.

3. Black bears are omnivores—they eat plants and meat. They mostly eat acorns, nuts, berries and other fruits, insects, green plants, and dead animals.

4. A group of bears is a sloth of bears **(C)**, but that's not the most accurate name for them since sloth comes from the word **slouthe** which means slow. And black bears are not slow. They can run up to 35 miles an hour—as fast as a car driving through a town.

5. They lose up to 25-40% of their weight over the winter **(B)**. That's why they stock up and eat non-stop all day long (except for an hour or two) in the fall before they hibernate.

6. No, black bears do **not** drink when they hibernate. They also don't eat, pee, or poop.

7. Black bear cubs are 17 months old **(B)** when mother bears shoo them away. A cub is born to a mother one winter and still hibernates with her the next winter, but then the summer after the second winter, mothers shoo cubs away to live on their own. It's time for them to have more cubs—mother black bears give birth every two years.

8. When black bears hibernate, their hearts slow way down to 8 to 22 beats per minute **(A)**.

9. Small—black bears hibernate in dens that they can barely fit into. Cubs and their mothers curl into a tight ball when they hibernate to keep warm.

10. On average a black bear lives to be 25 years old **(A)**. The reason most black bears die is because they are hunted by humans.

How many did you answer correctly?